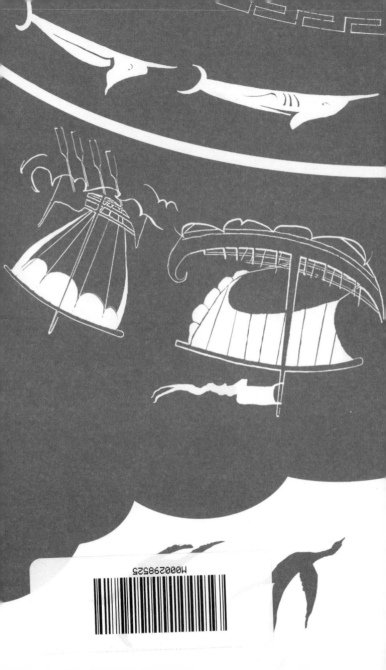

Tibor Fischer was born in Stockport in 1959, the son of refugees from the Hungarian Revolution. His first novel, *Under the Frog*, was rejected by 56 publishers before going on to be shortlisted for the 1993 Booker Prize.

Reading Fischer is a bit like watching *Reservoir Dogs*, or *Taxi Driver*: you are never quite sure if you're witnessing comedy or tragedy. Few writers have a better feel for the inventive set-up: the Hungarian Revolution from the point of view of the national basketball team (*Under the Frog*); life as narrated by a 5,000 year-old Sumerian bowl (*The Collector Collector*); a man who teaches himself to read two books at once (*Don't Read This Book If You're Stupid*) and a south London loser who decides to become a deity in Miami (*Good to be God*).

His books are philosophical in the proper sense of the word: they make you think about and question every assumption life is founded on, but only when you've stopped laughing. The two stories collected here are no exception. In 'Crushed Mexican Spiders', a women returns home to discover the key to her Brixton flat no longer works. 'Possibly Forty Ships' couldn't be further from the grime of South London. It begins with an elderly eyewitness being tortured to reveal the true story of the Trojan War.

Tibor Fischer lives in Brixton.

POSSIBLY FORTY SHIPS

By the same author

POSSIBLY FORTY SHIPS

Tibor Fischer

unbound

POSSIBLY FORTY SHIPS

This special limited edition first published in 2011

Unbound
21 Peter's Lane Clerkenwell London EC1M 6DS
www.unbound.co.uk

Typesetting by Bracketpress

Lettering and endpapers designed by
Ryan Gillard & Kiera Kinsella

Jacket photography by Hana Vojáčková

A CIP record for this book
is available from the British Library

ISBN 978-1-908717-03-0

Printed in England by Clays Ltd, Bungay, Suffolk

'You know how this works.'

'May I assure you that not only do you not have to torture me, you don't even have to bother threatening me with torture.'

'And may I assure you that I have no shame or hesitation in torturing a defenceless old man. So, talk.'

'How can I assist your curiosity?'

'You know. The war. The Trojan war. I'd like to hear the understory, the truth.'

'The truth? How do you define —'

'Let's not start that. I've heard the Stories and I've heard some stories. I've heard the ... talk ... I want the what-I-saw from someone who was there.'

'I was there.'

'You know what I'm asking. Everyone swears this was the greatest of the wars, everyone has heard the stories of the glories. Everyone says the heroes' names will be lip-ferried to the

9

future. Tell me about the War at Troy.'

'How do you define war? What is a —?'

'Chop two.'

'You still have some fingers left and a good chance of not bleeding to death.'

'Thank you. I didn't like those fingers anyway. And a man my age needs so few.'

'Let's start again. No word-fiddling.'

'The stories are … well, what everyone says about the war … they don't have much to do with what happened. The stories and the lived, they're as similar as, say, a horse and a leech.'

'The beginning?'

'Of course. Now if I were to point out every untruth, we'd be exhausted —'

'I'm in no rush.'

'First of all, probably, in all likelihood, the most important thing to say about the Trojan War is: there was no war.'

'No war?'

'Well, and please let me finish, because I honestly want to satisfy your curiosity, it again depends what you intend when you confer the title of war. If you see war as a few ships sinking in the middle of the waves, a few dozen warriors in armour, frankly not as gleaming as it could be, being welcomed whole-heartedly by the water, far, far away from Troy, if you see that as war, then it was a war.'

'Helen?'

'Helen's not a story. She was the wife of Menelaus. Good-looking, not that good-looking, but good-looking.'

'Paris?'

'Real.'

'And he abducted her to Troy?'

'Not in the widely accepted use of the word abducted. Menelaus forced her on Paris. He was bored with Helen; once you've had your wife in fifty-six positions, it's not the same, is it? Menelaus wanted Troy's wealth and an excuse. He told Paris he was divorcing Helen and he would consider her removal a courtesy. Paris was only up to position number five or so, so he cheerily agreed. And Paris returned to Troy with a barkful of wine, congratulating himself that Greek and Trojan relations were as happy as a mouse in a granary.'

'*And Menelaus got together an army of all the Greeks?*'

'A few of the Greeks. Have you ever asked anyone for a favour?'

'They all said they were there.'

'Afterwards, they all said they were there. Have you ever noticed how when something important or funny happens everyone pretends they were there? I was there when Kalchas ate a whole pig in one night. There were five of us there. Since then I must have met fifty people who insist they saw Kalchas eat a whole ox. Stories recruit. Give people what they want and you'll never go hungry.'

'*So Agamemnon and Menelaus set sail for Troy?*'

'No, not King Agamemnon. He sent floral encouragement.'

'*So the Greek fleet set sail for Troy?*'

'Again, it depends how you care to define

fleet, but we set sail for Troy.'

'And the fleet sank?'

'All but one ship.'

'How?'

'There are at least two ways of looking at this. Some would argue that Menelaus and his intimates were guilty of serial impiety and that the Gods meted out punishment by storm.'

'Or?'

'Menelaus was poor. As kings go, a beggar. The reason he wanted to loot Troy was not greed, but need.'

'Ornamentation is all. Only those who are poor at greed speak ill of it. What is the point of being in a world full of appearance, if you don't have the appearance you want? How will your greatness be known, if it can't be seen from afar?'

'Your greatness is unmistakably great—'

'My greatness doesn't require your notice. Back to Troy.'

'Menelaus owed a lot of money to Xanthos the Wine-trader. You owe a man one goat, it's your problem; you owe a man fifty good-yielding goats, it's his. Xanthos had concluded that the only way he would get any money back was by investing in war. So Menelaus's battle-fleet was really Xanthos's salesmen.'

'Not much in the way of preparation?'

'"Is this a good idea, going to fight Troy?" That thought was slinking around. But no one knew how well defended Troy was. One or two traders had been there. "So what's Troy like?" "They've got walls." Okay. "Have they got towers?" "How do you define tower? Yeah, they've got towers." So they have walls and towers. Does that help you much? "Are they moderately assailable walls or not?" "How do you define moderately assailable? I'm not sure, it was a long time ago. Maybe."'

'And why did you go?'

'I had nothing better to do. My brother had the goats, and I was a bean-grower whose beans shunned life.'

'This Xanthos was to blame?'

'No. Unless you count good sense as a crime. Out at sea, the weather turns nasty. You didn't have to be a bore of windlore to see this was bad.

Xanthos orders us to land. Menelaus who has been afloat twice, on a lake, says no, we can ride it out. Xanthos's crew, these old salts, they're so maritime, they're practically fish. They're terrified, some of them are crying like little girls, growing the sea. Menelaus's bodyguard, his favourite killers, they're terrified. They're doing everything to look like brutish bronze-drivers, but fears are bulging out of them like horns.

'You understand how when someone's really helped you, you really hate them? Menelaus hated Xanthos, because he owed him everything, and because he made money from wines of no fame. "People don't want good wine, they want bad wine, cheaply," Xanthos used to say. "Bad wine is, even if you piss into it – which I do – wine. You only go out of business worrying about quality." Menelaus countermanded Xanthos not because he thought he was right, but because he had to. The storm comes, and afterwards we're the only ship in sight, in a corpse and wreckage soup.

'No one said anything. There was much toe-gazing. Even for a king, it's embarrassing losing your entire army before the war starts, although army might be an over-generous epithet for the band of simpletons, thieves, fishermen, ne'er-do-wells and a pet seal under Menelaus's command. There was even one group who thought they were travelling to Egypt. They had paid a hefty fare.

'Finally, Menelaus breaks his silence. He has Xanthos weighted and thrown overboard. "That's the debts. Now, a slow story-building trip home," he proclaims. "It was Xanthos's impiety and recklessness that cost us everything. Any questions?" No questions. We're glad to be alive and heading home, all of us vowing never to leave land again. Then the lookout shouts that there are three ships approaching, with Trojan insignia.

'We're almost crippled, we can't outrun them and the storm must have pushed us into Trojan waters. "Listen carefully," says Menelaus. "There was no army. There was no war. We love those Trojans to profanity." I'll say this for Menelaus: he would have decapitated his mother for a bowl of fresh figs and he couldn't organise a cockfight, but he could lie from dawn to dawn.

'The Trojans board. They're no fools. Word has reached them about Menelaus. They see the floaters, but since Menelaus hails them like brothers, as brothers you actually like, they take him to Troy, which he maintains is exactly where he wants to go.

At Troy, we are greeted like dead rats in your water supply. The idea of slitting Menelaus's throat and using him as fertiliser is visibly given consideration. Maybe they admire the way he lies, but King Priam and the others listen.

Menelaus stands there and declares he came to Troy because he wanted a Trojan wife now that Paris has a Greek one. He adores their culture so much he wants to learn how to speak Trojan, to recite some of their great epics and to gorge on that famous Trojan fried pigeon. They listen to him, pondering fertiliszer.

'But he's their jug. And everyone has a sister or daughter they want to get rid of. They think about fertiliser and selling the rest of us into slavery, but maybe it's better to have a marriage of some sort. And if they kill Menelaus maybe, possibly, someone in Greece will seek revenge, or perhaps the deities of hospitality will be vexed. They marry Menelaus off to a very minor princess so ugly she has to sneak up on a fig tree to pick the fruit. They tattoo Menelaus with Trojan emblems, since he professed such admiration for Trojan culture, including one on his back, which, I was reliably informed, signified "I am Priam's jug." And they make him recite thirty lines of poetry every evening.'

'That's it?'

'Nothing happens for a long time. Menelaus doesn't want to go home. He realises he's a contender for jug of jugs. And, curiously, life at the Trojan court, even as a jug, isn't bad. He has all he wants, and the fried pigeon is, as they say, remarkably good. He becomes a very fat, very drunk fat drunk. The Trojans mock him mercilessly. They can't believe he's still draining their hospitality years after arriving. "You're sure you're not the Menelaus who said he was going to burn Troy?" "Lose any armies today, lard lord?" Priam joked that some rulers have pet lions, some have pet giraffes, I have a pet king. The court magicians used to work him into their displays.'

'And what were you doing?'

'I was retinue. Troy had its own bean-growers, so I had to tag on to the ankle of Menelaus. The great Belly-Grower said to me, "You. I don't know how long we'll be here or how I'm getting out of this, but we need some verses to cover our red, smacked arses. You, you'll be the wordwarden. We need a yarn when we get back. Get me some good stories and well-wrought epithets or I'll have you impaled. Meanwhile, I'll have a think about how to get out of this." He thought about it for six years.'

'So Troy's towers were untouched?'

'I didn't say that.'

'But you said there was no war?'

'You don't need a war to rase a city. It was six years after we had arrived. I was reconciled to dying there. I could have got back, but I,

19

like Menelaus, had nothing to go back to. I got a bit of fried pigeon every now and then, so crisp and yet so succulent, and I had done some work I was very proud of, creating Beta, a bare-breasted princess warrioress of Greece who has a six-year single-combat with Zeta, the bare-crotched princess warrioress of Troy, at very close quarters, if you follow me. Who doesn't like to hear about over-oiled women locking limbs? Well, Menelaus didn't. He felt it wasn't martial enough. Beta's sidekick was a wise-talking tortoise, but Menelaus didn't like the tortoise either. He had been bitten by one as a child.

'One day, Menelaus is staggering around the dock, more grape than man, as a Greek ship is putting out to sea. Some kid, eleven or twelve, on the deck spots Menelaus and makes this well-known gesture of contempt.'

'That one.'

'Menelaus goes mad. He's been snooked by the Trojan nobility every day for six years, but he has accepted this as a ruse in his master plan of revenge. This Greek kid is too much. He dives in and almost drowns trying to reach the ship, he wants to throttle the kid so badly.

'He summons his retinue. There are five of us left. Helen, of all people, helps us; her conjunctions with Paris aren't as regular as they had been. And Menelaus has an advantage in his plotting. He's a well-established buffoon no one in Troy takes seriously. He announces he's going home, but he wants to leave a present.'

'This wouldn't be the Trojan Horse?'

'How did you guess? Yes, Menelaus wants to leave an offering. Helen did the real work, she was very clever. It wasn't easy doing things unnoticed there, but as I said they'd stopped worrying about Menelaus. They had other, slimmer, more vigorous enemies, who were sniffing around in the distance with their chariots, prodding. We built the giant horse, as the stories relate.'

'But no warriors?'

'No one remotely heroic. Menelaus still had two bodyguards, but one had a bad back and the other was blind.'

'No Achilles then?'

'Ever meet anyone who knew Achilles?'

'Yes.'

'Then you can take pleasure in knowing they were shameless liars. Achilles was ... my private joke. A skinny child who liked wearing dresses. I scattered some truth in the stories. Any ten-year-old girl with spirit could have bested him. They only took him on the expedition because with so many men on a lengthy military campaign, they might need a jug.

'He reached Troy with us where he made clothes for the women. He was the only one of us exiles to be successful there.'

'And God-like Odysseus?'

'Odysseus was god-like. Powerful, good-looking, cunning, daring. The man all men would want to be. Of course, he never got to Troy.'

'What happened to him?'

'This I didn't witness. This is tittle-tattle, though my sources are trustworthy. Odysseus was with us in the storm, then ... no sign. What I heard was, after several misfortunes, he eventually adorned the King of Ethiopia's bed, pumped full of poppy and bummed into madness. He was there for some fifteen years. At the end they said you could drop a vole into his rear.'

'So he didn't want to get back to Ithaca?'

'Have you been to Ithaca? I'm not surprised he wasn't in a rush to return to kingship, to listen to someone complaining about their goat's yield being affected by their neighbour's incantations or someone filching some beans. The King of Ethiopia got tired of him or died. So he, the poppy-eater, had to go home. It's not surprising that none of his companions made it back from the Ethiopian court with reminiscences to offer around the fire during the long winter evenings. Nor is it a wonder he butchered everyone he found in his palace.'

'And how did the real Trojan Horse work?'

'We built it with fire-growing materials, it was stuffed not with soldiers but with hay, as a horse should be. We waited till the high point of the summer, when it was dry and hot, and we placed it next to the houses of the poor. A four-legged bonfire, ready for its flame.

'Menelaus wasn't in the mood to be hacked to death by irate Trojans, so his plan was to sneak away at night, to be already well out to sea, cherishing the distance and the darkness, while his army stayed behind and took the risk of igniting the Horse. The army was me and the bodyguard with the aching back.'

'Your loyalty was remarkable.'

'It depends how you define loyalty. The two of us were ordered, at the least wakeful moment of the night, to light the horse and as many buildings as we could. Then to rush to a boat through wrathful Trojans and row out to find Menelaus, waiting for us gratefully, in the middle of the dark. Not a proposition that guaranteed a tranquil old age.

'If I had refused, being the former lackey of an unpopular fat drunk in a foreign city who had tried to destroy it, that wasn't a very appealing proposition. On the other hand, carrying out the orders was suicide. At the last minute, as we stood in front of the Horse with our torches, the bodyguard with the bad back cursed his luck for not going blind and decided to go to the Trojans to squeal about Menelaus's treachery.

'It was strange. I was getting what I wanted when I had followed Menelaus: to burn down Troy. There I was, clutching a torch, with the opportunity to ash an entire city single-handedly with a single hand. I was getting what I wanted but in a way I didn't want. In a cowardly, despicable way, that would almost certainly bring me death. And even more exasperatingly, it wasn't just a cowardly way to attack your enemy, your hosts who'd given you some fried pigeon, not as much as you'd like … but it would be a cowardly, anonymous way.

'No one would ever know it was me, because Menelaus would seize any glory, and so even that small clique who admire perfidious arson and shameful murder, even that small clique wouldn't admire me.'

'So you chose to burn Troy? I'm looking at the man who destroyed Troy?'

'No, I did what most people do when faced with a difficult choice. I did nothing. I stood there with the torch, wondering. As my mind circled like a dog chasing its tail, the wind chased a spark into the Horse and that was that. I was knocked off my feet by the blast. I ran and I ran with an interest in running I'd never had before.

'I got to the boat and rowed out into the darkness. I didn't think I'd find Menelaus, but I figured it would be safest to be out at sea, that I might be picked up by someone who wouldn't kill me straight away. When I hit Menelaus's ship, I don't know who was more surprised, him or me. I could see the weighting-and-throwing-overboard order being given consideration. "Why aren't you dead?" he observed, doubtless thinking it would be inauspicious to kill a man with such luck.'

'Your fortune does seem to be good.'

'Men with good fortune usually have ten fingers and a plate of fried pigeon, Trojan style. Miles out, we could see the flames feasting on the city. We could see, whatever might remain, Troy was broken. Helen and Menelaus stood together like the old couple they were and watched a city burn, tired. It is a pity pleasure can't, like a stream, flow endlessly out of one person. There would be fewer burning cities.

'Bearing in mind I'd won his war for him, Menelaus could have said thank you in a brief, insincere, offensive monarch-like way, when no one was listening.

'I only have one real regret. I have my disappointments and I wonder how my life might have been if I hadn't embarked for Troy or if Menelaus the Fat-Gatherer hadn't been so stupid or if I had taken one of the trade routes out of Troy to see what was there; but that's the unknown, you don't know whether there's a friendly bosom or a rusty dagger lurking. I wish I'd been braver or cleverer, but my only regret is that I didn't tell Menelaus, more pig than man, to his face what I thought.'

'But then you wouldn't be here. What I don't understand, if what you say is true, is why didn't Menelaus make you, as the wordman, give him unlimited praise? Why does he take such little glory in the stories?'

'The fat hadn't softened Menelaus's mind. He wanted the story to grow, to hide the truth, so he told me to make him a spectator. He knew if the story was his slaughtering everyone, no one would swallow it, but this way he could be a small part, but a part of a glorious story. He knew he couldn't be greedy here, he had to give away the spoils imaginatively. Agamemnon and Odysseus and the many others who weren't there wouldn't refuse the glory of city-sacking, and no one could be too jealous of a hero like Achilles, who didn't exist and who was dead to boot. It's one thing to lose, another to see your hated rival win.

'They say a great God once came in disguise to a goatherd who gave him hospitality. In return, the God offered the goatherd any wish. "Ah," said the goatherd, "there is a man in the village who has a black goat. This goat is the envy of all, its milk flows day and night and is beyond compare. It makes the best cheese in the region. He is becoming rich from this one goat." What do you think the goatherd asked for?'

'Ten goats like the black one?'

'No.'

'Of course not. A thousand goats.'

'No. The goatherd asks for the black goat to sicken and die.'

'I grew up with the stories, old word man, and found no point to war because we were in infant battles, the crumbs fallen off the heroes' table for us ants. I sobbed because I couldn't have been at Achilles' side. My ambition was poisoning me, but now I can see the throne is vacant. Have you ever seen a real hero?'

'How would you define a hero? I would say someone who is cheerful when there is no reason to be cheerful invites admiration.'

'I wouldn't. Now to more important matters. Now your mouth can change history.'

'Tell a story that is wanted and it will stick to ears like tar. Tales of bravery are so popular, because that's as close to bravery as most of us will ever get. But, what is praised everywhere but welcome nowhere?'

'The truth?'

A NOTE ABOUT THE TYPEFACE

This book is set in 11 on 14pt Monotype Bembo Book. Originally drawn by Stanley Morison for the Monotype Corporation in 1929, the design of Bembo was inspired by the types cut by Francesco Griffo and used by Aldus Manutius, the great scholar-typographer of Renaissance Italy. In 1495, Aldus used it to print Cardinal Bembo's tract *de Aetna*, an account of a visit to Mount Etna. Not intended to be a facsimile of Manutius' work, Morison's Bembo was drawn to embody the elegance and fine design features of the original but marry them with the consistency of modern production methods so it would work with high speed printing techniques.

The Bembo used here is the new digital version, called Bembo Book, designed by Robin Nicholas and released in 2005. It is slightly narrower and more elegant than other digital versions of the typeface and was drawn to produce a closer match to the results achieved using the hot metal version when letterpress printed.

Jennifer Whitehead
Tim Whitmarsh
Cat Widdowson
Rob Widdowson
Richard Williams
Jon Wilson
Doug Winter
Emma Woolerton
Kevan Worrall
Simon York
Jon Young
Shahed Yousaf
Lynn Zarb
Jens Zwernemann

Philip Sanders
David Scally
Ralph Scott
Iciar Senovilla
Katie Shaw
Michael Silbert
Marion Sinclair
Nicolette Smallshaw
Steve Smith
David Somers
Kolja Stille
Hayden Strawbridge
Jon Sumroy
Rory Sutherland
Dave Taylor
Michael Terwey
Charles Testrake
Libby Thompson
Laura Thompson
Matt Thorne
Serena Tierney
Perrin Tingley
Stephen Vizinczey
Scott Wallace
Kate Webster
Richard Webster
Paul Whelan
Wynn Wheldon
Stephen White

Howard Noble
Graeme Nuttall
Daithi Ó Crualaoich
Gina Orchard
Daniel Paine
Rosie Parsons
Dorota Parsons
Adrian Parsons
Tibor Pataki
Eszter Pataki
Nicola Paterson
Thomas Patterson
Martyn Payne
Seb Pearey
Simon Pitt
Justin Pollard
Kyle Porter
Rachel Poulton
Ben Ralph
Stephen Reid
Patrick Reynolds
Mark Richards
Scott Robertson
Krisztina Rohaly
Kate Ruse
Dave Russell
Jenny Ryan
Paul Sadler
Wayne Saich

Robert Loch
Stephen Longstaffe
Simon Lucy
Simon Lyell
Andriy Mnih
John Macmenemey
David Malyon
Darlene Manthorpe
Sarah Massey
@Clintsmate
Ajay Mathur
Evelyn McElroy
Kate McFarlan
Ian McIntyre
Stuart McKears
Bob McLaughlin
Saul Metzstein
Bruce Millar
Sabrina Miller
Ronald Mitchinson
John Mitchinson
George Mitchinson
Hamish Mitchinson
Rory Mitchinson
Oyvind Moll
Bethan Moore
Andrew Morris
Michael Mosbacher
Amie Mustill

Dean Irvine
Richard Isherwood
Johari Ismail
Emily Ispanovic
Fadi Jameel
Jody Jeffcoate
Nick Jefferies
Ian Jindal
Sarah Johnson
Tim Jones
Erkan Kahraman
Lidija Katic
Yuri Katzevman
Andrew Kelly
Lewis Kershaw
Azam Khan
Kevin Kieran
Dan Kieran
John Kiernan
Narell Klingberg
Marta Korintus
Terry Lander
Ros Lawler
Charles Leigh-Pemberton
Brian Levine
Lisa Lewis
Helen Lewis-Hasteley
Carol Lindsey
Steve Lloyd

Rose Ferrara
Rachel Francis
Katharine Fuge
Nina Furu
Erik Gabor
Surrey Garland
Patrick Gatenby
Simon Gibson
Grant Gillespie
Richard Goddard
Sophie Goldsworthy
Esteban Gonzalez Torres
Emma Gordon
Ceri Gorton
Adam Grant
Louise Greenberg
Matthew Grice
Melanie Hancox
Craig Harper
Patrick Harrison
Martha Harron
Peter Hartman
Harriet Harvey Wood
Joanna Hawkins
Chris Hogarth
Alex Holliman
Helena Hollis
Metin Huseyin
Annie Kocur

Paul Cooper
Jessica Coppin
Duncan Corns
Alison Cowan
Sue Cox
Martin Coyle
John Crawford
Iain Cross
John Crowther
Martin Cull
Heather Culpin
Stephen Dabby
James Dasey
Cathy De' Freitas
J.J. DeGasky
Derval Devaney
Anthony Dickinson
Harry Dienes
Mark Dixon
Barbara Donoghue
Michael Downer
Lois Drysdale
Alison Dunn
Richard Eggleston
John Eustace
Michael Farquhar
Safron Faulkner
Charles Fernyhough
Cindy Ferrara

Suzanne Bath
Nick Bath
Bob Beaupre
Kenny Beer
Catharine Benson
Steve Berryman
Stephen Betts
Maureen Bode
Karl Bovenizer
Mary Bracht
Gareth Buchaillard-Davies
Jonathan Bullock
Chris Bunker
Nicholas Burton
Marcus Butcher
Richard Butchins
Miguel Calderón Alonso
Jim Cameron
Niki Campbell
Xander Cansell
Cynthia Carbone Ward
Richard Case
Claire Chambers
Zelda Chappel
Ian Claussen
Andrew Cogan
Tony Cook
Paul Cook
Lewis Cook

SUBSCRIBERS

Geoff Adams
Chris Addison
Wyndham Albery
Cassandra Arnold
Alice Barnsdale
Cath Barton
Jennifer Basch
Nikki Bateman
Naomi Bath

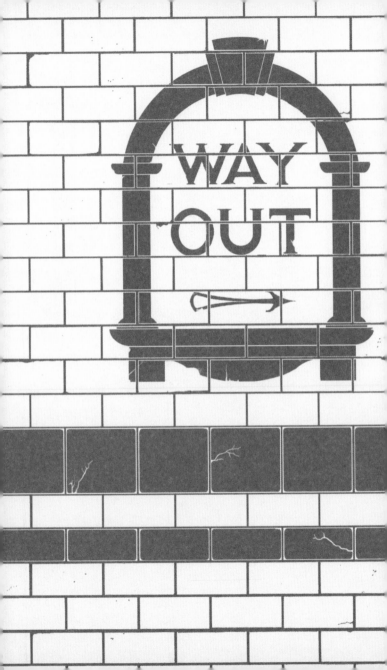

Tibor Fischer was born in Stockport in 1959, the son of refugees from the Hungarian Revolution. His first novel, *Under the Frog*, was rejected by 56 publishers before going on to be shortlisted for the 1993 Booker Prize.

Reading Fischer is a bit like watching *Reservoir Dogs*, or *Taxi Driver*: you are never quite sure if you're witnessing comedy or tragedy. Few writers have a better feel for the inventive set-up: the Hungarian Revolution from the point of view of the national basketball team (*Under the Frog*); life as narrated by a 5,000 year-old Sumerian bowl (*The Collector Collector*); a man who teaches himself to read two books at once (*Don't Read This Book If You're Stupid*) and a south London loser who decides to become a deity in Miami (*Good to be God*).

His books are philosophical in the proper sense of the word: they make you think about and question every assumption life is founded on, but only when you've stopped laughing. The two stories collected here are no exception. In 'Crushed Mexican Spiders', a women returns home to discover the key to her Brixton flat no longer works. 'Possibly Forty Ships' couldn't be further from the grime of South London. It begins with an elderly eyewitness being tortured to reveal the true story of the Trojan War.

Tibor Fischer lives in Brixton.

CRUSHED MEXICAN SPIDERS

By the same author

CRUSHED MEXICAN SPIDERS

Tibor Fischer

unbound

CRUSHED MEXICAN SPIDERS

This special limited edition first published in 2011

Unbound
21 Peter's Lane   Clerkenwell   London   EC1M 6DS
www.unbound.co.uk

Typesetting by Bracketpress

Lettering and endpapers designed by
Ryan Gillard & Kiera Kinsella

Jacket photography by Hana Vojáčková

A CIP record for this book
is available from the British Library

ISBN 978-1-908717-03-0

Printed in England by Clays Ltd, Bungay, Suffolk

Ahead of her, struggling up the stairs struggglingly, was a mother and pushchair laden with bags and a screaming kid. Homebound workers salmoned past without offering a hand, blinkered by visions of supper or respite.

The comatose staff of London Underground didn't think of helping the mother. She wouldn't be helping either. Ten years ago when she had moved to London, she would have. Imperceptibly but perceptibly the city toxified you. Parking across strangers' driveways, not saying thank you when a door was held open for you, murder. Somehow it got you.

London informed you that you got nothing for a lifetime of decency; not even a free glass of water. Not that behaving badly necessarily got you anywhere, but it was generally easier and more fun; and finally any career criminal from Albania or genocidist from Rwanda passing through London got the same medical treatment as you and better housing rights.

You didn't want to become the sort of person who didn't help an entoiled mother, but you became one. No one had helped her when she had needed it. And now her help muscles had withered away. Single mothers were especially annoying because of their dishonesty. Very few of them could hack it. They either leeched on friends and family, sucking in services and cash, or they botched it up while maintaining how coping they were.

Outside, on the pavement, a Portuguese junkie was kneeling, while a buxom exorcist wielding a bible intoned with two back-up entreaters and sprinkled him with holy water.

Sidestepping the adjuration she threaded her way through the clumps of beggars, drug-dealers, thugs and seething commuters that made up Brixton. She ran walking. To get home was all she wanted. The strength of the desire was almost alarming.

She had thought about getting out. She had been thinking about little else. And she hadn't just thought about it. Job applications. She was convinced she had sent more job applications

than any other human being. They had failed. She had written more. They had failed.

Then, while she would have been happy leaving London, her boyfriend couldn't. Harun worked as a junior information officer at the Turkish Embassy, and just as he was coming to the end of his tour of duty, after three years, when she had been counting on escape, teaching English and getting a tan and a family, they had split up. She knew you couldn't have everything. Harun farted a lot and always had to be infallible on international affairs, but had a sense of humour and was punctual. Now she was again at the mercy of London's nightlife.

What was a night out in London? Pleading your way into a club, past an ear-piece which had grown a moron. Once inside you had to fight to get served, and then your money went as if you were surrendering it to bandits. She had only managed to get the deposit on her flat because of her inheritance from her grandmother. Her grandmother hadn't been well off, but she hadn't been one for drinking, smoking, eating much, buying much, going

to the cinema or indeed anywhere. She played bridge with old friends and was of a generation that worked or starved.

Everywhere she went, on holiday or on business, was better. Dublin, Copenhagen, Istanbul, St Ives, St Petersburg, Palermo. You name it, it was an improvement. You'd walk into a shop and the proprietor would say hello instead of assessing how much you would be attempting to steal. Everyone she knew talked of leaving London. Somewhere calmer. Somewhere greener. Somewhere sunnier. Somewhere else.

As she approached her house, she could see the lights on in the ground-floor flat that belonged to Gloria. Gloria, who had a doctorate on the subject of slums in poor countries, and whose flat reflected that. Her parents paid the bills, and Gloria had sex noisily with embarrassed men who were never seen more than twice.

In the basement flat were the Cooks, an elderly couple who had been living there for forty years; they effortlessly annihilated all the myths about the nobility of the white working

class. They were sullen, smelly, fans of any manifestation of ugliness. Living in shit was evidently no problem for them, since they did nothing about the rubbish amassed, shin-high, in front of their door. For the first year she had greeted them, and been ignored. Twice, clandestinely, disgusted by the filth, she had gathered up the debris around their door. But then she gave up. Londoned.

The first floor was Rolf. An old, failed actor who lived on his own, he never had friends dropping by, because he was a bedridden inconsiderate miserabilist: a bedridden inconsiderate miserabilist, however, who had been an inconsiderate miserabilist long before he was bedridden. Yet he would never be one of those pensioners discovered long after the arrival of decomposition, because he was too unpleasant. A file of social workers shambled up to his flat, grimacing but reliable.

When she had moved in she had listened politely to Rolf's stories of being stranded in Ethiopia, playing third lackey in a film that had run out of finance, and explaining why he had

to keep a pool table in the hallway, a full-sized one that made it difficult for the other residents to get past.

In his favour Rolf was at least under her flat. His bathroom regularly flooded Gloria's flat, but he wouldn't do anything effective about it. It was fascinating how you could not care at all about others and still be cared for. One summer when she had worked at a giant campsite in Normandy she had noticed how the decent customers got the nightmarish reps and how the decent reps got the nightmarish customers. Invariably the nightmarish reps never got the nightmarish customers any more than the decent reps got the decent customers.

Then, up on the second floor, she saw traces of light in her flat. Even though she assumed she must have left a light on in the morning when she left, she couldn't suppress a creep of anxiety. This was a city where everything was done to guarantee the liberty of burglars.

Although no one was watching her, or would be able to make her out in the dark, she felt ridiculous as she fumbled with the key in the top

lock. The lock had never given her grief before, but no matter how many times she slipped the key in, it refused to turn. After several minutes of failure, it occurred to her that the locks must have been changed, so persistent was the lack of turning. Had there been a burglary during the day? If the locks had been changed why wasn't there a note? She chose to ring Gloria's bell to see what was going on.

Over the intercom, a male voice answered.

'Good evening,' she asked. 'Is Gloria there, please?'

'No Gloria here.'

Had Gloria moved out? Gloria had been in the house when she moved in, but they had never got on. She had first met Gloria fifteen minutes after she had magazined one unbelievably large hairy spider and given another unbelievably large hairy spider a taste of the nine hundred and sixty-six pages of the telephone directory. She had been agitated, because they were too big to be London spiders.

'I'm Gloria. You haven't seen two largish spiders have you?' Gloria, it transpired, bred

spiders. She had always thought it was blank males who collected exotic or venomous creatures to make themselves more interesting or to feel powerful because they had one of the only five Armoured Mist frogs in the world stashed under their bed, as one suitor in a pub had recounted to her.

She had directed Gloria to the spider paste. 'Kelvin. Melvin,' Gloria had obituarised. 'I let them out for exercise,' she explained when asked how they had escaped. The hatred that Gloria had launched had been quite unjustified and unbalanced and relations hadn't much improved.

'Have the locks been changed?' she asked. 'I'm in the second floor flat and I can't get in.'

'No one's changed the locks,' the male voice insisted.

'Could you let me in please?'

'I don't know who you are.'

There was a receiver-replacing conversation-terminating clack on the intercom. She pressed the other buttons, but no one responded. In the darkness she could just perceive that the

names by the buzzers on the intercom looked different, but she couldn't make out the letters. She wondered what to do. Wait for someone to go in or come out? Call for a locksmith? It was cold.

As she wandered out into the driveway, she looked back up at her flat and she saw a woman at the window looking down at her. Shocked, she didn't quite know how to react. The interloper was a woman at the wrong end of middle age, unlikely to be a burglar, but very possibly mentally ill. The interloper was unfazed, observing her for a few moments before slowly retreating to the inner reaches of the flat.

She hit her own buzzer: 'Who are you?'

'Sorry?'

'What are you doing in my flat?'

'I don't know who you're looking for, but this is the second-floor flat.'

'I know. I've lived in it for seven years.'

'No. I've lived here for seven years.'

'If you don't let me in, I'll call the police.'

'If you don't go away, I'll call the police.'

'This has gone far enough.'

'This has gone far enough. If it's your flat why is it that I'm in here and you're out there?' Another conversation-terminating clack.

Was this some elaborate practical joke? Television chicanery? She looked around for concealed chucklers. If it were a joke, she would exact terrible revenge. She retrieved her phone from her bag, but, to top it all, it wouldn't work. Gagging with rage she strode over to the nearest pay phone and called the police. After hanging on for several minutes, she explained that someone was in her flat. She then paced up and down in the driveway for twenty minutes, past the orange bathtub that had been there for months, and which, certainly, would be there for months to come. Eventually the police shot past with the sirens going. A few minutes later, they drove back and stopped in her driveway.

Two police officers emerged from the car with that caution police officers exhibit in case someone starts shooting at them. One was a policewoman who must have been the result of some Equal Opportunity mania, almost a dwarf,

tubby and with a look that said she couldn't believe she had been accepted for the job. The other was a towering, wall-wide veteran to whom she re-explained her predicament.

The police drew down the woman in her flat. Her name was Mrs Gardiner. Her name was inscribed by the bell. Mrs Gardiner swiftly produced correspondence from utility companies that enthroned her as the rightful occupant. The mystery man from the ground floor flat maintained Mrs Gardiner had been living there for years. They went upstairs to the flat – Rolf's pool table had vanished – where her claim that the curtains in the back bedroom were red was proved wrong. All her belongings were gone. The flat had been totally redecorated, refurnished.

She was asked to provide any evidence that she lived there. She could have sworn she had a letter from her bank in her bag, but it was gone. Mrs Gardiner now studied her with the compassion reserved for the mentally ill who have just done something awful to themselves. The policeman couldn't have been more

sympathetic as tears bunched in her eyes.

'I'd like to help,' said the policeman. 'But you see how it looks. This lady has proof of residence. You don't. Your keys don't fit any of the locks. The neighbours say they've never seen you before. Are you on some medication?'

Mrs. Gardiner commented, 'She needs help.'

The rage and the weariness made her leave. She couldn't bear to see how they looked at her. She didn't know what to do. She walked over to the nearby newsagent run by a barely counter-high Asian woman who greeted her.

'You know me, don't you?'

'Of course,' the newsagent replied, but as soon as she replied she realised that she would have said the same thing to a complete stranger.

'Do you know what's going on over the road?'

'What's going on over the road? Something's always going on over there.'

Mechanically she started walking towards the underground. She'd deal with this tomorrow. Stay with someone tonight and get on the case tomorrow, but none of her friends lived

in the area. She tried her phone again: still not working. Stopping at the only working payphone, she tried her friends. The first attempts produced no reply. Then when she phoned Don, who was almost the last person on whose sofa she'd consider sleeping, a non-Don voice answered.

'Could I speak to Don?'

'You've got a wrong number.'

She punched the number again, extremely slowly to make sure she got it right, but only got the non-Don voice.

She took the tube back into Victoria and went into the first okay-looking cheap hotel. All she wanted to do was curl up. The receptionist ran her credit card and then announced it was no good. With only a few pounds in cash, she went out to the cashpoint on the corner, and after she had tapped in her number three times, the machine ate her card.

It was now gone eleven and she took stock of how badly she stank. She made another round of phone calls. The numbers were unavailable, no one was there or an unfriendly voice would

deny the person she was looking for. Finally, she returned to her office hoping to spend the night there, but when her key froze in the lock of the front door she wasn't surprised.

There was one last call to make, the one she dreaded most of all. When a strange voice answered her parents' number, she knew they were gone as well.

She caught the last train back to Brixton, and in the passageway between the two platforms, she sank down and gave way to tears.